From the mouth of the bottle appeared the yellowed edge of a slip of paper. With his small fingers, Sam pulled it out partway.

The paper was dry and crumbly. It looked burned around the edges. Sam looked at Polly. She was staring at the paper with round eyes.

"You pull it out the rest of the way," Sam said.

Polly put the bottle down on the sand. As carefully as Sam, she pulled the parchment completely out of the bottle. She unrolled it.

"Yes!" she said.

"What? What?" asked Sam. "What does it say?!"

Polly's eyes glowed when she turned to him. "Three wishes."

Water
Wishes

THE FIRST BOOK IN
The Magic Elements
Quartet

by Mallory Loehr

A Stepping Stone Book™

RANDOM HOUSE 🏠 NEW YORK

J
Loe

For my father, who loves the sea

Text copyright © 1999 by Mallory Clare Loehr.
Cover art copyright © 1999 by Elizabeth Miles.
All rights reserved under
International and Pan-American Copyright Conventions.
Published in the United States by Random House, Inc., New York, and
simultaneously in Canada by Random House of Canada Limited, Toronto.

www.randomhouse.com/kids

Library of Congress Cataloging-in-Publication Data: Loehr, Mallory.
Water wishes : magic elements quartet / by Mallory Loehr.
p. cm. — "Book one." "A Stepping Stone book."
SUMMARY: While staying at the beach for the summer, ten-year-old Polly
and her younger brother Sam find a message in a bottle, providing them
and their thirteen-year-old brother with exciting and scary adventures.
ISBN 0-679-89216-8 (trade) — ISBN 0-679-99216-2 (lib. bdg.)
[1. Beaches—Fiction. 2. Wishes—Fiction. 3. Brothers and sisters—Fiction.]
I. Title. PZ7.L826113Wat 1999 [Fic]—dc21 98-49558

Printed in the United States of America 10 9 8 7 6 5 4 3

Random House, Inc.   New York, Toronto, London, Sydney, Auckland

A STEPPING STONE BOOK is a trademark of Random House, Inc.

Contents

---~~~~~~~~~~~~~~~---

Prologue

*I*n a cave below the sea, something wakens. It stretches and gazes lazily about. It does not want to work. It wants to play.

The water shivers as a bottle rises from a rotting treasure chest. A voice whispers into the bottle. A light fills the cave for a moment, then winks out.

The bottle is gone, too...

CHAPTER ONE

~~~~~~~~~~

The Problem with Joe

Sam saw the bottle first. It was bobbing on the waves, fat and shiny and green.

"Hey!" he shouted. "Look!"

Polly looked up from the sand castle she was building. What was Sam shouting about? Then she saw the bottle glowing in the bright sunlight.

"Get it, Sam!" she called. She climbed to her feet and ran to the edge of the water, spraying sand in her wake.

Joe brushed the sand off his comic book. He

looked over his sunglasses at his brother and sister and shook his head. He was thirteen and the oldest.

"So what?" he muttered. "It's just an old bottle." He went back to reading his comic.

Polly was ten years old and Sam was seven. Sometimes they tried to be cool like Joe. But not today. Today they didn't even *think* about strutting back to their towels. They'd been on vacation for two days and they were ready for something to happen.

Sam and Polly splashed into the shallow water. They stayed even with the bottle as the waves carried it down the beach. Slowly, they went deeper into the water, breaking their parents' "Knee Rule"—kids don't go in water over their knees without a grownup around.

The bottle kept bobbing just beyond where the waves were breaking. But as much as they wanted the bottle, the two kids were careful about not going out that far. Waves that seemed gentle and rolling were another story once you were in them.

Polly and Sam were starting to get tired. Despite the motion of the waves, the bottle wasn't getting any closer. Just as they were ready to give up, a giant wave came surging toward them.

"Yikes!" said Sam.

He and Polly ran.

Polly was a fast runner, especially when something was after her. The wave hit her in the knees. She stumbled, but kept going.

Sam was not so lucky. The wave crashed over his head and smashed him into the sand face-first. Everything swirled around him. He couldn't tell which direction was up. He couldn't breathe. The water pulled at him, tugging him under.

Sam thought he was going to drown, but then a hand grabbed him.

"What's the matter with you guys?" said Joe, depositing Sam on the sand. "You know the Knee Rule. If you can't keep it, you're going to have to stay in the house. You could have drowned."

Sam coughed up sea water.

"You're just lucky that I followed you," said Joe. "Come on, kids. It's time for lunch."

"You're a kid, too, you know," Polly said as they started to walk back along the shore.

Joe ignored her as he carefully draped his towel over his arm.

"What about the bottle?" Sam asked.

He and Polly turned to look at the waves.

The bottle was gone.

Polly sighed. "I just know there was a genie in there," she said wistfully. "I could just see him, sitting on sea-foam pillows, waiting for us to let him out."

"Yeah," said Sam.

Polly looked at Sam.

"You should have kept your eyes on it better, Sam," she said unfairly.

"It's not *my* fault," said Sam, even though he almost never won arguments with Polly.

"Yes, it is," said Polly.

"No, it isn't," insisted Sam.

"Yes, it—" began Polly.

"Be quiet, you guys," said Joe. "Can't you *ever* stop it?"

Polly and Sam both glared at Joe.

"You're not Dad," said Polly.

"You're not Dad," echoed Sam.

Polly elbowed Sam and they both giggled.

Joe gripped his towel tighter and tried to ignore them.

Sam and Polly shared a room with bunk beds. Polly had the top bunk. Sam didn't mind. He was afraid he wouldn't be able to climb down the ladder in the dark if he had to go to the bathroom. The next morning, Polly and Sam got up early. As soon as each made sure that the other was awake, they scrambled out of bed. They made a quick detour to the bathroom before running upstairs.

In the kitchen, Uncle Ned was making fancy coffee. Aunt Sarah was reading the paper and feeding Little Ed. Little Ed was eating and throwing things. Their father was making waffles and singing silly songs. Polly and Sam sang with him as they set the table.

Their mother came up the stairs while they were singing. She yawned, then smiled sleepily at everyone. That was one of the best things about the beach vacation—no one said to be quiet, even early in the morning.

Uncle Ned passed Mom a cup of frothy coffee.

Little Ed shouted, "No!" and threw a piece of banana.

"I was *never* like that," said Sam as he and Polly finished setting the table.

"Amazingly enough, you weren't," said Mom. "But Polly and Joe were."

"Maybe Joe," said Polly, "but not me."

"Speaking of whom, why don't you two go wake up your big brother," said Dad as he poured pancake batter on the hot griddle. "I'm sure he'd be happy to hear your melodious singing."

Polly and Sam looked at each other and grinned. They galloped down the stairs. Then Polly stopped.

"Wait," she said. "Let's sneak in real quietly. When we're right next to him, we'll shout, 'Wake up!'"

"Yeah," said Sam.

Joe's room was cool and dark, the way he liked it. In past years, the three kids had shared a room at the beach. This year, however, Joe had declared himself too old to share. Surprisingly, their parents had agreed.

Polly and Sam crept into the dark room. Joe was a lump in the bed. The air conditioner made a whooshing sound. Sunlight slanted through an opening in the heavy shades. Sam noticed the light made a weird green glow on Joe's dresser. He looked closer.

It was the bottle.

Sam nudged Polly. She gasped. They stood frozen in the middle of Joe's room. Polly jerked her head to the door. Sam nodded. They crept back out, not quite as slowly or as quietly as they had gone in.

"Did you see it?" Sam whispered.

"Of course, silly," said Polly. "What I want

to know is, how did Joe get it?"

Polly and Sam thought about this for a moment.

"It must have been when he rescued me from the wave," said Sam. "Maybe when he pulled me up."

"Yeah," said Polly. "He must have been close behind us. I can't believe we didn't see him."

"I'm glad he was there," said Sam.

"We would have been fine without him," Polly said. "It's not like we really were drowning. And it's *our* bottle. We followed the bottle and Joe followed us. So the bottle's ours."

Sam didn't point out that it was really *his* bottle because he saw it first.

"Okay," said Polly. "Here's the plan. We sneak back in and get the bottle. Then we hide it."

"And then we have to wake up Joe for pancakes," Sam reminded her.

"Of course," said Polly, "but we take care of the bottle first."

Slowly, Polly opened Joe's door. She and Sam peeked in.

The room was still dark. Joe hadn't moved.

Carefully, they tiptoed across the room. When they were halfway to the dresser, Sam bumped into Polly. It was a quiet bump, but they both froze. Polly glared at Sam.

Joe turned over and made a snuffling sound.

Polly and Sam held their breath. Joe didn't move again.

Polly waved her hand at Sam to tell him to wait. He did. He didn't want to make her too mad—not after the bump.

Polly crept the rest of the way over to the dresser. She reached out to the bottle. Her fingers closed around the neck. Then—

"JOE! TIME TO WAKE UP, YOU SLEEPYHEAD!" Dad bellowed from the kitchen.

His voice boomed through the open door into the quiet room.

Polly and Sam watched in horror as the dark lump that was Joe rose up.

CHAPTER TWO

~~~~~~~~~~~~~~~

The Hiding Place

*J*t only took Polly a moment to realize that Joe's eyes were closed. She whipped the bottle behind her back. The next few seconds seemed to happen in slow motion.

Sam came up behind Polly.

Joe stretched out his arms.

Polly handed the bottle off to Sam.

Joe yawned.

Sam pivoted toward the door.

Joe's eyes opened.

Polly stepped forward to block Joe's view.

Sam fled, the bottle clutched to his chest.

Joe blinked when he saw Polly right in front of him.

"Good morning, darling brother!" she cried. "We're having pancakes! You'd better hurry if you want some."

Then she turned and ran. Joe leaped out of bed and ran after her. Polly looked back and screamed. They went laughing and screaming up to the kitchen.

Sam heard them. He wondered if Joe was torturing Polly to tell him about the bottle. He nearly took the bottle out of its hiding place so that Joe would stop.

Then Sam decided that Joe wouldn't really hurt Polly. He would get in too much trouble. And Joe was usually pretty nice for a big brother. It was just that he used to be a *fun* big brother. Now he was too busy being cool. Sam missed the old Joe. He thought Polly did, too, which was why she pestered the new Joe so much.

Sam looked down at the laundry basket full of dirty beach towels. It would have to do as a hiding place for now. At least the bottle would be well padded in there.

After breakfast, Joe had to wash the dishes. Sam and Polly were relieved. It meant that he wouldn't find out that the bottle was missing for a while longer.

Sam and Polly handed all the dishes to Joe as fast as they could. He hated doing the dishes—especially without a dishwasher—but he had lost the argument with Mom.

Just when Polly and Sam were heading off to look at the bottle, Mom called out to them.

"I hate to tell you, but we've got to have a little clean-up this morning," she said.

Sam and Polly groaned.

"None of that," said Mom. "Ned and Sarah have gone to the grocery store with Little Ed. And your dad's out looking for next year's house, as usual. Since Joe's doing the dishes so nicely, it's your job to tidy the living room a bit. All you have to do is stack the toys and games and books."

"But, Mom—" began Polly.

Mom held up her finger. "*And* straighten your rooms."

"But—" was all Sam managed to get out before Mom gave him "the look." He knew what that meant.

"Okay," he said.

Mom ruffled his hair.

"You're a good one, Sam," said Mom.

Polly rolled her eyes.

Mom kissed her on the head. "You too, Polly-o."

Polly rolled her eyes again.

Mom didn't pay any attention to the eye-rolling. She just turned and called into the kitchen, "Thanks for doing those dishes, Joe. I love you."

Joe grunted and shrugged his shoulders.

Mom shrugged her shoulders, too, with a sad smile on her face.

Sam and Polly picked up their stuff in the living room.

Joe finished the dishes. He stomped down to his room.

Sam and Polly crouched at the top of the stairs, waiting for him to come out yelling. Instead, he came out with a comic book and his sunglasses. Sam and Polly looked at each other. Polly wiggled her eyebrows at Sam, who had to cover his mouth to keep from laughing.

Sam and Polly watched as Joe went out to the beach. They were only a little envious as they cleaned up their bedroom. It was fair, after all. Joe was so neat that his room hardly ever needed to be tidied. Also, Sam and Polly now had time to figure out what to do with the bottle.

Just then, Mom poked her head in the door.

"We've only been here three days, and we're already out of beach towels. I'm going to do laundry, so give me any dirty clothes," she said.

Polly thought quickly. Sam had told her

where he'd hidden the bottle, and she didn't want to lose it again.

"Um, Mom?" said Polly. "I don't mind using dirty towels."

"Me neither," said Sam.

"Yeah," Polly continued, "don't you think you've worked hard enough? You need a break. In fact, don't worry at all. Sam and I will do the laundry."

"I can't believe what I'm hearing," Mom said. "What's going on here?" She leaned down and looked first Polly, and then Sam, in the eye. They both tried not to laugh at her playfully stern expression. Their mother straightened back up with a laugh. "You goofy kids. I don't know what you're up to. All I want is your dirty clothes."

"No, wait," said Polly. "Seriously. Don't you think it would be a good idea if we learned to do laundry? I mean, what if something happened to you? Isn't laundry a good thing to know? I wouldn't want to grow up wearing dirty clothes. And neither would Sam."

"No way," said Sam, holding his nose.

"Kids never cease to amaze me," Mom said, gazing skyward. "Okay, you win. Laundry lessons it is. You can start by bringing me your dirty clothes."

Polly and Sam each gathered a pile of dirty clothes and towels. They carried them to the washing machine, which was right outside their bedroom door. Over her armload of laundry, Polly saw Mom lifting a towel from the top of the laundry basket.

"Stop!" shrieked Polly.

Mom dropped the towel. She stared at Polly.

"She doesn't want to miss a single step," Sam said seriously.

"I guess not," said Mom. She looked at Polly sideways. "Are you sure you feel okay, Pol?"

"Yes," Polly answered. "It's like Sam said. I just don't want to miss anything."

Mom looked doubtful. "All right, if you say so." She picked up the towel again. Polly's mouth opened. Mom's eyebrows rose. Polly's mouth shut.

"I'm explaining," said Mom. "This is called 'sorting.' You sort out the lighter colors from the darker colors. You wash them separately. That way the dyes from the darks can't bleed into the lighter colors. Remember the time Joe did the laundry and everything turned pink? That was because he threw everything in together, and the dye from a red shirt in the laundry colored everything that was lighter."

"Yeah," said Polly, "I remember. You had to buy him new underwear. I get the dye thing."

"Yeah, it's cool," said Sam. He nodded knowingly.

Mom had a funny expression on her face, but she went on bravely. "It's very cool. So, we'll mostly have darks in this load because beach towels are usually bright. Now, how about you two sorting the laundry while I put the soap in the washing machine?"

Mom waited for Polly and Sam to want to

know how to add the soap. But they were already sorting.

Mom turned and shook her head.

Behind Mom's back, Sam held up the bottle. He put it behind his own back.

"Um, Mom?" Polly said.

"Yes?" asked Mom, still measuring soap.

"I think maybe we've learned enough about laundry for today."

Mom looked at the half-sorted pile. She sighed and put the measuring cup down. Sam and Polly looked hopeful.

"Oh, go on," said Mom. She waved her hands at them. "Shoo."

"You're the greatest mom," Polly said.

"Ever," said Sam.

Mom bent down to finish the sorting.

Sam and Polly ran up the stairs.

Mom looked after them.

She shook her head for the millionth time and went back to the laundry.

CHAPTER THREE

The Message

The sun disappeared behind a cloud as Sam and Polly ran out of the house.

They were ready to run down the stairs, along the wooden walkway to the beach. Then they saw Joe down on the beach. They could see him bobbing his head to music from his Walkman and singing into a rolled-up comic book. It would have made them fall down laughing if they hadn't had other things on their minds.

Instead, Polly just said, "Other way," and

they doubled back and went out the front door. High dunes blocked the view of the sea and rock star Joe.

Sam and Polly crouched between the dunes, out of sight. They looked at the bottle.

The bottle had a fat belly. The neck was a couple of inches long, with a cork stuck in it. The glass was a deep green with a perfectly smooth surface. But it looked darker and duller than it had before.

Polly frowned. So did Sam.

"I thought it was lighter," she said. "Or maybe I mean brighter."

"It was," said Sam. "And it looked like there was something in it."

"Really?" asked Polly.

Sam nodded.

"Hmm." Polly turned the bottle over in her hands. "Should we pull the cork out?"

Sam looked unsure.

"Are you scared?" Polly asked.

Sam shook his head, but it was a little shake.

Polly grinned. "Maybe something will come out in a big puff of smoke. And grow bigger and bigger, until it's a giant monster with huge fangs and spiky claws..."

Sam stuck his lower lip out.

"I don't believe you," he said. "I think there's a genie in there who will give us three wishes."

"Oh, do you?" said Polly, forgetting that she'd said the same thing. "Then here"—she held the bottle out to him—"you open it."

Sam waited a minute before he took the bottle. He cradled it in his arms. Then he grabbed the cork and looked up at Polly. Her eyes were wide. For all her teasing, he could tell she expected something to come out, too. Finally, he closed his eyes and pulled.

The cork came out with a hollow *pop*.

Sam and Polly stared at the bottle.

A faint mist seemed to rise out of the opening. Then it blended with the air and was gone.

Sam and Polly waited.

Nothing happened.

Sam looked into the bottle. He couldn't see anything. He closed one eye and pressed the other against the mouth of the bottle. All he could see was blackness. He shivered.

Polly held out her hand. Sam passed the bottle to her. She looked into it, too.

Polly sighed. "Oh, well! So much for magic."

Sam frowned and rubbed his cheek with his shoulder. He was too disappointed to speak.

"I hate that," said Polly. "Just when you think something special is finally going to happen."

Sam nodded sadly.

"Sam, what if nothing magic ever happens and then I get like Joe?" Polly asked.

Sam looked alarmed. "You won't be like Joe," he said. "Will you?"

"I don't know," said Polly. "It just seems like weird things happen to you when you get older. Know what I mean?"

"Yeah," said Sam. "But Mom and Dad aren't like that. Not really anyway."

"You're right," said Polly, smiling. Then her face fell again. "Maybe it's just when you're in the middle. You know, in the middle of growing up."

Sam thought for a while as Polly stared at the dull bottle. "You'll be *you* if you want to be," he said finally.

"Maybe." She stood up. "I'm going to throw this bottle as far as I can, okay?"

Sam nodded.

Polly corked the bottle. She drew her arm back, then snapped it forward. The bottle flew into the air. And as it did, the sun came out from behind the clouds. The bright light shone through the bottle. For a moment, they saw a black shape outlined inside.

The bottle landed with a *thunk* beyond the dunes.

The two kids peeked over the dune at the beach. Joe was still there, reading his comic and moving to the music. It would take a tidal wave to disturb him. A second later, Polly and Sam were flying over the sand toward the place the bottle had fallen.

Polly grabbed the bottle. She pulled out the cork and turned the bottle upside down. She shook it, but nothing came out.

"Here, use this," said Sam, handing her a dry reed.

Polly poked the reed into the bottle.

"It touched something!" she said. "Kind of like a piece of paper."

"I bet it's a secret message," said Sam, "or a treasure map!"

"Maybe," said Polly. "Oh, I want to get it out."

She shook the bottle harder.

"Let me," said Sam.

He held the bottle up to the light. Then he poked the reed into it. He could see a roll of paper.

"I see it!" he said. "I think I can get it."

"Do you want me to hold the bottle for you?" Polly asked.

"Yeah," said Sam.

Polly held the bottle as Sam carefully

worked the reed into the center of the roll. Then he pressed it against the side of the bottle. Slowly, he pulled. From the mouth of the bottle appeared the yellowed edge of a slip of paper. With his small fingers, Sam pulled it out partway.

The paper was dry and crumbly. It looked burned around the edges. Sam looked at Polly. She was staring at the paper with round eyes.

"You pull it out the rest of the way," Sam said.

Polly put the bottle down on the sand. As carefully as Sam, she pulled the parchment completely out of the bottle. She unrolled it.

"Yes!" she said.

"What? What?" asked Sam. "What does it say?!"

Polly's eyes glowed when she turned to him.

"Three wishes."

"Really?" asked Sam. "Really, *really?* Three wishes?"

Polly nodded. "Yeah. I know, I can't believe it either. Maybe it's a joke."

"No," said Sam. "It can't be."

"Well, I hope not," said Polly.

"What does the rest say?" Sam asked. "Read it to me."

Polly held the paper so the sun fell on it.

The letters seemed to ripple in the sun. The ink was neither blue nor green, but both colors at once, in a shifting way.

The writing was not cursive, but something like it. The letters had points and curves in strange places. And the words got smaller and smaller as they went down the page.

Polly read it out loud.

Three Wishes
Whosoever pulleth
this page from the bottle
shall be granted
three wishes of this element.

"What's an 'element'?" Sam asked.

"I think it's just an old-fashioned word," Polly said. "It doesn't really mean anything."

"Oh," said Sam.

Polly read on. She pointed to the words so Sam could follow. The next part was in smaller letters.

Read the rules in fine print.

"What's 'fine print'?" Sam asked.

"It means the writing's nice," Polly said. "You know, it's *fine*."

"Oh," said Sam, looking at the flowing words. "I hate rules."

Polly did, too.

She read the smallest words on the page:

Rule 1: No wishing for more wishes.

"Oh!" said Polly. "Shoot." It was exactly what she had always planned to do in this situation.

"Keep going," Sam urged.

Rule 2: Wishes work only in the element noted.

"What's 'element' mean?" Sam asked again.

Polly ignored him and continued reading.

Rule 3: You can't keep what you wish for.

"That's it?" Sam asked.

"That's it," said Polly. "Three rules for three wishes."

"What about that?" Sam asked. He pointed to the ink at the bottom of the page.

"Oh, that's just a design," said Polly, "to make it even fancier."

Sam looked at the design. It looked like little waves. And the waves seemed to be moving! Sam looked away. He felt dizzy.

Polly was staring out at the ocean. The rest of the family had joined Joe on the beach with umbrellas and chairs. The clouds had disappeared completely.

"Let's plan the wishes," said Polly.

"Why can't we wish right now?" said Sam. "I know what I want."

"I've read too many fairy tales where people are stupid," said Polly.

"But—" said Sam.

"Remember the story about the guy wishing his wife had a sausage on her nose?" Polly continued. "That was a dumb wish. We wouldn't want to wish something by accident, then have to use our other wishes to fix it."

"Okay," said Sam. But he thought about what Polly would look like with a sausage on her nose.

"Great," said Polly. "We'll think about it and wish after lunch."

As they walked back to the house, Sam wondered how Polly had gotten to take charge of the bottle...

CHAPTER FOUR

Rotten Wishes?

After lunch, Polly and Sam went into their room to talk about the wishes.

Polly pulled the bottle from the pocket of her raincoat in the closet.

Sam got the rolled parchment out of his underwear drawer.

They placed the bottle and paper in the center of the room.

Polly got out a drawing pad and a pencil.

"Let's make a list of what we want to wish for," she said. She turned to a blank page on the drawing pad and got her pencil ready.

"To fly," Sam said quickly.

"That's a good one," said Polly. She wrote it down:

> Flying

Then she added:

> Famous
>
> Money
>
> Beauty

"But you can't keep it," said Sam. "That's the rules."

"I know," said Polly, "but I thought we could at least try. Those things can be really helpful. Like if Mom and Dad had money, they wouldn't have to work and we could live at the beach all the time."

"Put down 'toys' then," said Sam, "and 'new car,' so Mom and Dad can *both* have a car."

Polly wrote:

> Toys
>
> New car

Then she also wrote:

Never grow up

"Okay," Polly said. "That's enough to start. Let's choose one."

"Can we *please* try flying first?" Sam asked.

"Fine," said Polly generously.

Sam smiled. Then he looked puzzled. "How do we do it?"

"I don't know," said Polly. "Put a hand on the bottle and a hand on the paper. And then wish."

Sam followed her directions. Then he closed his eyes.

"We wish to fly," he said.

They waited. Sam stood on his tiptoes to see if he would rise up in the air. Nothing happened.

"Maybe we have to start it somehow," said Polly.

"Let's jump off the bed!" said Sam.

They spent a long time jumping off the bed. Nothing happened, except that Sam bruised his knee and nearly cried.

"Well, let's try another wish," said Polly finally.

Sam was sad about not getting to fly, but they didn't have a choice.

"I wish to be beautiful," Polly declared, a hand on the bottle and a hand on the paper.

Sam looked at her. Polly looked back.

"Can you see anything happening?" she asked.

"Nope," said Sam. "But I think you're already beautiful."

Polly went and looked in the mirror.

Her brown eyes looked back at her. Her straight brown hair hadn't gained a curl or a golden gleam. Sometimes she wished her hair was blond and wavy and her eyes were green, like lucky Sam's. Polly stared deep into her own eyes and remembered that she looked like her grandmother—the most magical person she knew.

"Oh, well," she said with a shrug and a smile. "Being beautiful is not that important. I didn't want to waste a wish on it, anyway."

Sam agreed. Together they looked glumly at the bottle. Then Sam had an idea.

"Polly," he said excitedly. "Maybe it needs to be in the sun! Remember how it was just a plain boring bottle until the sun came out?"

"You're right!" cried Polly. "I should have thought of that."

Polly and Sam grabbed the bottle and paper and ran outside.

On the dunes, Polly and Sam repeated their wishes. They still didn't work. Then they tried wishing for different things in different ways.

Polly threw the bottle in the air and wished for a dog.

Sam held his breath and wished to be stronger than Joe.

Polly whispered a secret wish into the bottle.

Sam balanced the bottle on his head and wished to go to the moon.

Nothing worked.

Sam and Polly sat in the sand. They were

too tired to wish anymore.

"I guess that's it," Polly said. "It's just a joke—a really mean joke."

"Maybe it's just not right yet," Sam said hopefully. "Maybe we didn't read it right. Maybe we got the rules wrong. Let's look at the paper again."

They unrolled the paper. Everything looked the same. Polly read it out loud until they both knew it by heart.

"I can't figure it out," Polly declared. "I might as well wish to be a mermaid or something *really* silly."

Suddenly, a terrible roar filled the air. Polly and Sam looked up. The sea looked as if it was boiling!

On the beach, everyone was gathering up towels and chairs and heading back to the house. Sam and Polly tried to get up, but they couldn't move! The waves got closer and closer. Finally, a giant wave flung itself up on the dune.

The water reached out foam-tipped fingers

to them. One finger grew longer and longer until it gently touched Polly's big toe.

There was a giant thunderclap, and rain started pouring down. Sam found he could move. He took off down the dune. But Polly was still sitting on the sand.

"Come on, Polly!" Sam shouted. "We've got to get inside!"

"I can't!" she screamed through the rain.

Sam ran back up the dune.

"What's the matter?" he asked.

Polly pointed down.

Her legs were gone. In their place shimmered the silvery blue-green tail of a fish.

CHAPTER FIVE

Tail Tale

Sam stared at the tail, then looked up at Polly's face. He couldn't figure out if she was crying or if it was the rain.

Then she laughed.

"It works, Sam!" she crowed. "It works!"

Just then, a voice rang out. "SAM, POLLY! GET INSIDE IMMEDIATELY!"

They both looked up. Their dad was standing on the deck of the house.

"How are you going to get inside?" Sam asked.

Polly stopped smiling.

"POLLY, SAM, WHERE ARE YOU?" Now their dad sounded worried.

"I'll get Joe," Sam decided.

Polly wrinkled her nose, but she didn't say no.

"Coming!" Sam shouted to Dad.

Polly made a shooing motion at him. "Quick! I'll be fine out here for a while. The rain is wonderful."

Sam ran toward the house.

Polly looked down at her tail and shivered with excitement. She ran her finger along the shining scales. It was weird. Her scales felt cold to her fingers, and her fingers felt hot to her scales.

Polly flapped the tail experimentally. She decided that, except for walking, she didn't miss her legs at all. The tail felt so much stronger than her legs ever had.

Polly looked through the rain toward the choppy waves. She closed her eyes and imagined how the water would feel, the tug of the tide pulling her in. Below the waves, the sea would be still—not like the stormy surface.

As a mermaid, she wouldn't have to worry about breathing underwater—she would breathe the water itself. Or were mermaids, like dolphins and whales, mammals that had to come up for air? Well, she could figure that out once she was in the water. She had to get to the water. She could feel it calling to her.

Polly thought crawling seemed undignified, but she didn't see any other way to do it. She rolled over onto her stomach. Slowly, she started pulling herself over the wet sand toward the waves crashing on the shore.

The door slammed behind Sam as he ran, dripping, to Joe's room.

"Hey, you're getting my floor wet!" Joe said, looking up from his comic book. But he pulled his earphones off to hear what Sam had to say.

"You've got to help Polly get inside," Sam said.

"What are you talking about?" asked Joe.

"Get Polly first!" Sam said.

Joe gave Sam a hard look. Then he swung his legs over the side of the bed and got up.

Sam told him where Polly was while Joe put his raincoat on.

"I'll go, but you'd better go upstairs and tell Mom and Dad you're here," said Joe.

Sam knew they were probably in trouble.

Outside, Joe forged his way through the rain to the dune. Polly wasn't there. Those kids had tricked him. *The little brats!* He was turning back to the house when a movement on the beach caught his eye. He couldn't make out what it was through the rain. But he could see that it was moving toward the water. Could it be a person? What if Polly had somehow fallen down the dune?

Fear gripped him. He ran down the dune. As he got closer, he recognized Polly's purple T-shirt. She had a shimmery towel wrapped around her legs. And she was pulling herself forward with her arms.

"What's going on?" Joe shouted as he

reached his struggling sister.

Polly looked up at Joe through the pelting rain.

"I have to get to the water," she said.

"What are you talking about?" yelled Joe. "We're in the middle of a storm. You can't go into the water. Mom and Dad would kill you."

"No, Joe, I really have to," she told him. "The rain isn't enough. I just have to get to…"

"Come on, Polly. Get up. Let's go," Joe said. "I'm not playing games. You can fool Sam, but you can't fool me."

"No, really," said Polly. "I can't walk. I'm a mermaid and I need to swim. Help me get to the water."

"You have *got* to be kidding," Joe said. "Go ahead, pretend you're a mermaid if it makes you happy, but you're going back to the house even if I have to carry you."

Polly looked at the crashing waves. They were reaching for her. But so was Joe. He bent down and got one arm under her shoulders and the other under her legs. He was amazed by how much they really *did* feel like a tail.

Luckily, Joe was strong for his age, and the house wasn't far. He half carried and half dragged her over the sand. The short flight of stairs to the bottom floor was the hardest.

When they got inside, Joe let Polly go. She dropped to the ground and glared up at him. She pointed to her tail.

"Look!" she said. "I *told* you."

Joe gaped. Slowly, he crouched down beside Polly and ran his finger over the scales.

"Wow," he said. "*Wow.*"

Polly smiled.

Upstairs, they could hear voices. Then Sam's rose loudly above the rest.

"Polly's in the bath," he almost shouted. "She was cold."

Polly and Joe looked at each other. Joe grabbed Polly under the arms and dragged her into the bathroom. He had to get in the tub himself to pull her in.

Frantically, Joe turned the taps up as high as they could go. Polly poured a whole bottle of bubble bath into the water.

"I'll go see if I can stall them some more," Joe said. He ran out of the bathroom.

Polly sat in the tub and watched as the water and bubbles slowly covered her tail. It felt delicious.

Polly lifted her tail out of the water and admired the shiny scales. They were silvery blue when she turned the tail one way and silvery green when she turned it the other. She splashed it to make more bubbles.

Suddenly, the bathroom door opened. It was Mom. Polly plunged her tail beneath the bubbles and tried to look innocent.

"Polly," said Mom, "what is going on? Stop splashing. You're getting water everywhere. Why do you have your T-shirt on in the bathtub?"

Polly looked down. She'd forgotten to take it off.

She looked back at Mom. "Oh, that..." she said, thinking hard. "That's because...because..."

"Because…?" Mom prompted.

"Because Sam and I were playing a game," Polly said. It was partly true, she figured.

Mom lifted an eyebrow as Polly squirmed. "And that's why we didn't know where you were and why there's water all over the place?"

Polly nodded.

Sam's head appeared in the doorway. He took one look at his mother and ducked out.

"We're sorry," Polly said, hanging her head. She sank deeper into the tub. She closed her eyes. The water felt so good. She wondered if it might be better with a little salt added.

"Polly?" her mother said, a note of concern creeping into her voice.

Polly's eyes snapped open. "What? What?" She'd forgotten where she was for a moment.

"Are you sure you're okay?" Mom asked. "You look a little spacey. Maybe it's time to get out of the hot water."

"NO!" said Polly, startling both her mother and herself with her forcefulness. Then she added as normally as she could, "I'd like to stay in just a little longer. Please? I love the water."

The bubbles were touching the rim of the tub. Mom turned off the faucets.

Mom smiled softly. "I know what you mean." She had a faraway look on her face. Then she looked back at Polly. "But take off that T-shirt. And you kids are going to have to clean up all the water in the hall."

"I know," said Polly. "We will."

Mom gave Polly a stern look. Then she went out, shutting the door behind her.

Back in Sam and Polly's room, Joe was pumping Sam for information.

"How did Polly get that tail?" Joe asked.

Sam wasn't sure how much to tell.

"Come on," said Joe. "Tell me what's happening. I know you and Polly were playing some kind of game. But this...this is more than a game."

Joe's eyes were shining. He looked so excited that Sam couldn't hold back.

"It was the bottle," he said.

"What do you mean, 'the bottle'?" said Joe.

"You know," said Sam. "The *bottle* from the *ocean*."

"What?" said Joe. His mouth dropped open. "You took *my* bottle."

"*My* bottle," said Sam. Then he added, "Mine and Polly's."

"Wait one second," said Joe. "*I* was the one who pulled it out of the water. You guys were too busy drowning."

"Yeah, but—" began Sam.

"I just can't believe that you would sneak into my room like...like..." Joe couldn't think of anything bad enough to compare his brother and sister to. "I just can't believe—"

"It wasn't like that—" Sam interrupted.

"And what's the bottle have to do with what's happening?" Joe went on. He towered over Sam. "Huh?"

"Well," Sam said, "it gave us three wishes. There was a piece of paper and rules to follow and everything and we tried to make them work and they didn't. Then Polly wished to be a mermaid and...and...she *was* a mermaid!"

Just then, they heard Polly. She was calling quietly from the bathroom.

Joe's mind was spinning with a combination of excitement about the magic and resentment at not having been a part of it. He closed his eyes and took a couple of deep breaths.

"We'd better go help her," he said. "But don't forget, I want to know everything. *Everything.*"

Sam nodded, grinning.

Polly was sitting on the bathroom floor, wrapped in a towel. She was staring at her tail, which shimmered brightly. She looked up with a hopeful expression when she saw Sam and Joe in the doorway.

"I didn't want to get out," she said. "But I thought that you could help me down to the ocean."

"No way," said Joe. "I don't care if you *are* a mermaid. It's dangerous out there. We'll help you to the bedroom."

Polly frowned. "But there's no water there."

"Grab an arm," Joe told Sam.

They pulled Polly into the bedroom.

"I want to be by the window," she said.

"Yes, Your Highness," said Joe.

"Can you open the window?" Polly asked as she settled into the chair.

"But it's raining," said Sam.

"I know," said Polly. "I want to feel it."

"Being a mermaid is making you crazy," said Joe.

"You're just jealous," Polly said, sticking her tongue out at Joe.

Joe looked at her and shook his head. "You're only a mermaid because you stole my bottle."

"It's not yours," Sam broke in.

As Joe turned to glare at Sam, Sam quickly added, "Don't you want to know about the wishes?"

Joe looked wearily from Sam to Polly and back again. "Yeah," he said. "Explain."

So Sam and Polly explained. Actually, Sam did most of the talking because Polly had a hard time turning away from the window. Joe listened to it all with a hungry expression on his face.

When Sam got to the part about finding the parchment, Joe wanted to see it.

"I guess it's still out *there*," Sam said, pointing to the window.

"Maybe I should get it," Joe said. "What if it gets lost?"

There was a crack of lightning, quickly followed by a roar of thunder. Salty rain blew through the window.

Polly lifted her face to it and sighed.

Joe shut the window.

"NO!" said Polly.

"The floor's getting all wet," said Joe. "Aren't you in enough trouble already?"

Polly pressed her wet face to the window. She sighed again, but seemed a little more alert.

"I don't think you should go out," said Sam. "Besides, I know exactly what it said." Sam repeated the words on the parchment.

Joe shook his head. "It's incredible!" he said.

Sam realized that he could ask Joe a few things that had been bugging him. "What are elements exactly?"

"A long time ago people called fire, water, earth, and air 'elements,'" Joe said. "And 'the elements' sometimes means weather or things like iron and oxygen."

"Water," said Polly. "It's got to be."

"Yeah," said Joe, "I think so, too."

"Okay," said Sam. "Now tell me what 'fine print' means?"

"'Fine print' means the smallest words," said Joe.

"We read those," said Polly.

"Tell me the rest," said Joe.

Polly told him about all the wishes they'd tried. She and Sam started to laugh when they thought of trying to fly. Joe watched them giggle hysterically.

"Stop it," he said sourly. "Tell me the next thing!"

They told him about the rest of the failed wishes and then how the bottle had seemed dead until the sun hit it.

"That must be part of the magic," Joe said. "You need sunlight."

Finally, they got to the part about the mermaid wish.

"And you know the rest," said Polly. "Now can I go out?"

Joe looked thoughtful.

"How close to the ocean were you when you made the wish?" he asked.

"Not that close," said Sam. "We were up on the dunes."

"Could you see the water?" asked Joe.

"Yeah," Sam and Polly said together.

"I bet that's part of it, too," Joe mused. "Water is the element, and you have to be in its presence."

Sam was impressed.

Joe looked back from Sam to Polly. "You know," he said, "if you'd told me about it to begin with, I could have helped."

Just then, the lights went out.

"Uh-oh," said Sam.

Polly flapped her tail.

"Wait here," said Joe.

He felt his way to the door. He opened it and waited for his eyes to adjust to the darkness. He could hear people moving around and bumping into things upstairs.

Suddenly, a faint golden glow bloomed at the top of the steps.

"Ta-da!" said Dad. "Candles! Just in time for a lovely dinner!"

"Kids!" called Mom. "Dinnertime!"

Joe went back to Sam and Polly's room. "Did you hear that?" he asked.

Polly was pulling her nightgown over her head.

Joe groaned. "This isn't fair," he said. "You took *my* bottle, I have to rescue you from the beach and now I have to carry you!"

Mom appeared in the doorway, holding a candle.

"Come on," she said. "I'll lead you upstairs."

Sam and Joe made a seat for Polly out of their arms. Mom's eyebrows rose.

"What's this?" she asked.

"We're playing that I'm a mermaid princess," said Polly airily.

"Joe too?" Mom asked, surprised.

"We couldn't do it without him!" declared Sam.

Joe rolled his eyes. "No kidding!"

After dinner, the wind died down and the rain beat softly on the windows. They all played board games in the living room by candlelight. The lights came back on while Mom was reading *Peter Pan* aloud.

Polly kept her tail covered with her nightgown the whole time. When it was time for bed, Dad carried her downstairs.

"You feel like a real mermaid!" he said.

He tucked Polly and Sam in, and Mom kissed them good night.

Light came in through the window. The storm had stopped. The clouds had cleared. The moon was almost full.

"Water," Polly whispered sleepily.

"Polly?" said Sam. "Do you think we'll get

another wish tomorrow?"

But Polly had fallen asleep.

Sam closed his eyes. He drifted off to the sound of Polly's breathing, which rose and fell like the waves.

In his own room, Joe stared at the ceiling. The magic had given him some ideas of his own...

CHAPTER SIX

Stolen Wish

The next morning, the sun rose slowly from the ocean, turning the clouds pink and gold. A green bottle sat on the high dune where, the night before, a mermaid had lain. A tattered piece of paper rose like frozen smoke from the bottle's neck.

A lone figure walked onto the dune. A tanned hand picked up the bottle and pulled the paper out. The figure walked toward the water, holding the bottle and the paper.

A moment later, a giant wave washed over the shore. When the wave withdrew, the figure was gone. All that remained was the parchment and the bottle. The bottle cast a long green shadow onto the sand behind it. The paper was again tucked into the bottle's neck. But a few things were different.

Sam woke up as Polly climbed down the bunk bed ladder.

"Your legs are back!" he said.

"Yeah." Polly didn't sound too happy about it. "And I didn't even get to swim."

"You got to take a bath," said Sam.

She frowned. "It's not the same," she said.

"Let's go find the bottle and make a wish!" said Sam.

A few minutes later, they were creeping upstairs to grab something to eat. Uncle Ned heard them and turned away from the window.

"Weather's weird," he said. He took a sip of his fancy coffee, his eyes going back to the window.

Polly and Sam went and looked out, too.

The sun was hanging just above the water. Clouds fanned out from it. The sky was blue.

"Uh-huh," said Polly. She didn't see anything weird.

"Look at the waves," her uncle said.

"Yikes," said Sam.

The waves were rolling in quickly. They seemed to be coming from far away and got bigger and bigger until they rose up and crashed on the shore. Spray flew everywhere. Even at a distance, the waves looked huge.

"Think I'll find the weather on TV," said Ned.

"Um, Uncle Ned?" said Polly. "Sam and I are going to go outside for just a bit."

"Fine with me," said Ned. He turned on the TV and began flipping through the channels. There was a lot of static. "Just don't get too close to the water. I don't trust it today."

"We won't," Polly and Sam said together.

Polly and Sam each took a bagel from the kitchen, then they headed outside. The sunlight made them squint and the wind whipped sand against their legs.

They made their way over to the high dune where the magic had first worked. The bottle wasn't there. Polly and Sam looked around while the blowing sand burrowed into their clothes. Polly's hair was heavy with it and Sam's mouth tasted gritty.

"There it is!" Sam shouted against the wind.

Polly had to shield her eyes to see where he was pointing. The bottle sat on the sand near the water.

They ran down the dunes. The sand stung their skin relentlessly, but they didn't notice. Instead, they gaped at the waves. At close quarters, the waves were even more enormous. The sound they made was huge, too. It looked as if the waves would swallow the bottle at any moment. But, somehow, they seemed to keep washing up on either side of it.

Sam and Polly hung back and took in the scene.

"We've got to make a dash for it when the waves go back," Polly shouted.

Sam looked at Polly with a terrified expression. Polly looked back out at the giant waves. She straightened her shoulders and lifted her chin.

"I'll go," she said. "I run faster. Besides, it's kind of like jump rope."

"Be careful," said Sam.

He watched as Polly nodded to the rhythm of the waves. Suddenly, she took off, making a beeline for the bottle. Sam loved how fast she could go. The waves rose like walls around her, but they didn't touch her. She snatched up the bottle and turned to head back.

"Run!" screamed Sam.

A wave loomed over her in pursuit. Sam ran, too. Polly caught up with him just as the wave came down behind them with a crash.

"That was close," said Sam. He was breathing hard.

"But we got it!" said Polly. She held up the bottle in victory.

"Yeah!" said Sam. He looked at the raised bottle. "Wait," he said. "Something's different."

Polly lowered the bottle and they both looked at it. Water sloshed inside the bottle like a little ocean, complete with waves and a sandy bottom. But the strangest thing of all was the tiny pair of sunglasses floating on the surface.

"Uh-oh," said Sam.

"Joe," said Polly. She stared at the little sunglasses. "He took our bottle. He took our wish."

The wind blew her hair across her face. The salty strands stuck to her cheeks and eyelids. She peeled them away with her hand. Her eyebrows were lowered and her shoulders hunched as she turned her glare away from the bottle and out at the surging sea.

Sam didn't know what to say. He didn't know why Joe had done it. He watched as thoughts rose and fell in Polly's eyes, waiting for her to figure out what to do.

"He took one of our wishes," she repeated.

"I can't believe he is such a jerk. He just thinks he's so great." Polly's eyebrows lowered into a scowl.

"How do you know he used a wish?" said Sam.

"Of course he used a wish," Polly growled. "That's why his sunglasses are in the bottle. How else could it happen?" Her voice got louder. "He thinks he's *so* grown-up. Grown-up Joe can do whatever he wants!"

Sam didn't have a chance to say anything before Polly went on, her eyes looking far away.

"That's it," she said, quietly and ominously. She grabbed Sam by the shoulders and looked into his eyes. "We're going to have to disown him."

"Okay," said Sam, glad a decision had been reached. "We'll disown him." He paused. "What's 'disown'?"

Polly rolled her eyes. "It means that we'll never speak to him again. And if someone says that he's our brother, we'll say no, he isn't."

Sam looked at the bottle again and the

tiny sunglasses being tossed about. "But…
but…what if Joe's in trouble now?"

"What?" Polly snapped. "What do you
mean, 'What if Joe's in trouble?' He *is* in trouble. He's in trouble with me—" Polly stopped
talking as a thought occurred to her. She smiled
slowly. "I have an even better idea. Joe is going
to be in trouble with Mom and Dad, too. He
didn't tell anyone where he was going. He
broke the rules. Just wait until they find out."

"But…but…" Sam gulped. "I meant, maybe
he's in danger-trouble. Like he needs to be
rescued."

"Rescued?" said Polly. "Rescued? Use the
last wish to rescue him? He got himself into
this. I refuse to waste a wish rescuing him." And
with that she turned and marched back toward
the house, tucking the bottle under her sweat-
shirt. At the door she turned back and shouted
to the sky. "I never want to see him again!"

A crack of lightning lit the sky as Polly tore
open the door to see her mother staring at her.

"That's not a nice thing to say," Mom said.

"But it's true!" protested Polly.

"Be careful what you wish for," replied her mother with a faint smile. "Siblings, any siblings, aren't easy," she added, seeing Polly's expression. "Why don't you go on upstairs? The table needs to be set."

"Why do *I* always have to set the table?" Polly asked.

"You don't," her mother said mildly.

Polly ignored her. She lifted her chin. "I have to get something out of my room."

"And then you're going upstairs to…" Mom prompted.

Polly rolled her eyes. "…set the table. I know. I will. Geez."

Back on the beach, Sam's eyes drifted to the giant gray-green waves. He felt very small. He wondered where Joe was. He wasn't sure that Polly was right and he *was* sure that something was very wrong. But he didn't know what he could do about it. And he didn't know if they were supposed to be disowning Joe or getting him in trouble.

"Come on in, Sam," his mother called.

Sam lowered his head against the wind and headed toward the house. He reached the top of the stairs in time to hear his father say that the pancakes were ready.

Polly was setting the table while Mom got out plates. Aunt Sarah put Little Ed in his high chair. Uncle Ned tore himself away from the TV and put butter and syrup and jam on the table. Finally, everyone sat down.

Sam smiled tentatively at Polly. She stared at him blankly, then turned to Dad.

"Shouldn't I go wake up Joe?" she asked.

Sam knew which plan Polly was going with now. But something was wrong.

The grownups were all just staring at Polly.

Little Ed screamed with glee and threw a pancake on the floor.

Finally, Mom spoke. "Who on earth are you talking about?" she asked.

CHAPTER SEVEN

No Joe

"Joe," Polly repeated. "You know...*Joe*...my big brother?"

"Heavens," said Mom, "I thought you outgrew your imaginary brother years ago, Polly!"

All the adults hid their smiles.

Polly felt her cheeks grow hot. She turned to Sam.

"The bottle," he mouthed at her.

Polly's face went from red to white.

Suddenly, their mother turned serious. She reached out and touched Polly's arm. "Are you feeling all right?" she asked. "You haven't seemed…yourself almost since we got here."

"Um, uh, no," Polly answered. "I mean, yes. I mean, can I please be excused?"

"Okay, Pol," said their mom. "Why don't you go lie down? Maybe we should take your temperature. You look really dreadful."

"Me too," said Sam. "I want to be excused, too."

Sam and Polly got up shakily from the table and went downstairs.

"I know," said Polly. "We'll go check his room. I bet he's asleep and they're playing a joke on us."

"Yeah," said Sam hopefully.

Polly and Sam crept into Joe's room. It was dark. But they could just make out a lump in the bed. Impatiently, Polly switched on the light. But instead of Joe, a teenage girl squinted at them from the bed.

"Natalie?" Polly's voice came out in a squeak. "What are *you* doing here?"

Natalie was their favorite babysitter, but

she hadn't sat for them since Joe turned thirteen.

"What are you talking about?" Natalie mumbled sleepily. "I drove up here with you guys to help your folks and Sarah and Ned." She rubbed her eyes. "What kind of game are you playing?"

"Nothing," said Sam quickly. "No game."

"No game," repeated Polly, backing up and turning off the light. "Sorry."

Their mom came down the stairs. "What are you two whispering about?" she asked. "And what are you doing out of bed?"

"I feel better," said Polly.

"Me too," said Sam.

"Well, okay," said their mom. "But maybe you should stay inside until lunch. It's looking a little stormy out. Why don't you get a game from upstairs?"

"We will," said Polly. "I just have to find something."

"Me too," said Sam.

Sam and Polly headed back into their

room. They shut the door and looked at each other.

"What's happening?" Polly asked Sam.

Sam shrugged miserably. "I don't know," he said.

"Shhh," Polly hissed, her face still pale. "I'm thinking."

Polly went to the closet where she'd stashed the bottle and pulled it out. She lifted it up, and they both stared at it.

"He's really gone," said Polly. "Totally."

"I told you something was wrong," said Sam. "We have to help him."

Polly glared at him.

"When you turned into a mermaid you wanted to be in the ocean really badly," Sam said. "Remember?"

"Of course I remember," said Polly. "So?"

"So, maybe it has something to do with that," said Sam. "Joe *did* get in the ocean. He must have. And now it won't let him go. And we're the only ones who even remember him, so we *have* to do something."

He looked sideways at Polly to see if she agreed. He thought it would be great to save someone, even Joe, even though he'd stolen a wish.

"You're wrong," Polly said. She'd just remembered something. "We don't have to do anything. My wish only lasted until the next morning. I bet tomorrow everything will be back to normal and Joe will be here complaining more than ever. And we'll only have one wish left."

Sam breathed a sigh of relief. "Yeah. I bet that's what will happen." He was disappointed that Joe didn't need them after all, but he wasn't sure that he could have convinced Polly to be part of the rescue operation.

The rest of the morning they stayed inside and watched as the sunlight dwindled away behind dark clouds. Uncle Ned had reported that the weather guys on TV were in an uproar. The weather was going haywire, they said. The winds and the tides were completely unpredictable.

By the afternoon, the world was gray. Gray skies, tall gray waves—even the sand was gray. Sam and Polly walked around on their deck, the cold wind whipping their hair into their eyes. Sam couldn't help still feeling worried. Polly couldn't help still feeling a little mad.

They all went out to a restaurant for dinner, which was a special treat. But Polly and Sam didn't feel very hungry. Natalie and their father both joked a lot, but it didn't raise their spirits. Uncle Ned did not stop talking about the weather. He was convinced they'd need to be evacuated before the end of their vacation. As they drove back to the beach house, rain had begun to fall. When they turned on the car radio, they heard the news that a hurricane warning had gone into effect.

That night, as Sam and Polly fell asleep, it was again to the sound of raindrops.

CHAPTER EIGHT

Hurricane Cain

The next morning, Polly and Joe woke up with a feeling of expectation. They bounded into Joe's room and pounced on the figure under the covers. Polly had her mouth open ready to yell at Joe when a very grouchy Natalie emerged.

"You've gone off the deep end," she grumbled at them. "Go back to bed. It's too dark to get up."

She was right. It was very dark. Sam and

Polly soon found out why. The hurricane had arrived, and its name was Cain.

Cain battered the beach house from all sides. The TV weatherman kept saying how unusual it was to have a hurricane in June.

Sam and Polly talked about what to do about Joe. Sam thought Polly wasn't worried enough.

"There's nothing we can do," Polly said. "No sun, no wish, no Joe."

Despite the lack of Joe, there was something thrilling about the hurricane. They stood at the window and watched as the rain seemed to blow in all directions at once. Sam even thought he saw it raining *upward* one time. Finally, Polly got bored and went off to read her book.

Sam kept watching. The wind whistled and whipped at the windows. The waves washed up to lap at the stilts beneath the house. Sam thought that if Joe were there, he would make up a story about how he'd created the storm with his powers over the weather. He hoped Joe was okay wherever he was.

Cain raged all through that Thursday and into Friday. Sam tossed and turned all night, dreaming about being caught under the waves. Polly dreamed about being a mermaid again.

On Friday morning, Sam and Polly were both feeling out of sorts when they woke up. Sam was sleepy and Polly was mad all over again about not getting to swim in the ocean. Sam told Polly about his drowning dreams, but she wouldn't listen to anything bad about the water.

After breakfast, Sam tried to get Polly to talk about what they were going to do about getting Joe.

Polly turned on him. "There's nothing we can do. We have to wait for the storm to go. And then we'll talk about it. Okay? Now leave me alone!"

Sam didn't say another word to Polly. He went to find his plastic knights. He staged elaborate rescue scenes all over the downstairs hall until Little Ed nearly ate a knight.

By the afternoon, the excitement of the storm had completely worn off for the whole family.

"I guess we should consider ourselves lucky not to be evacuated," said Mom.

"I don't know if 'lucky' is the right word," said Uncle Ned.

"Remember, we did have four nice days," Aunt Sarah said cheerfully as Little Ed howled.

"Two and a half," grumbled Dad. "We got here halfway through Saturday. Then there was that weird storm in the afternoon on Monday. Then Tuesday was cold and windy. Wednesday the rain began. Thursday and Friday, hurricane. Isn't that two and a half days?"

"It's all about whether the glass of life is half full or half empty," chirped Aunt Sarah. "We must all try and set a good example for the kids."

"Oh, leave him alone, Sarah," laughed Mom.

Dad looked at Aunt Sarah without saying anything. Polly had been watching the conversation. Dad's expression looked very familiar to her. It made her think of Sam.

Polly got up from the couch and went to look out the window. She knew she hadn't been nice to Sam. It was just that he kept bugging her about Joe. And Polly didn't think it was that bad without him. Or was it? Polly sighed.

She went to find Sam.

He was in their room, lying on his bed staring out the window. He scrambled up when Polly came in. He brushed his cheeks with his hands.

"Are you crying?" she asked.

"No," said Sam.

"Sure?" said Polly.

Sam's eyes filled with tears. "We're never going to be able to get him. We don't even know where he is or *anything*."

Polly stared at him. "I don't know," she said slowly. "Is it really so bad without him? Think about it, Sam. Isn't it great to not have anyone telling you what to do?'"

Sam looked at Polly in horror.

"How can you say that?" he said. "And it's not true anyway. It's not. You just like it because now you get to be the boss." Sam's face had turned bright red. "No one tells *you* what to do. You're being the same as him anyway." Tears had spilled over as Sam spoke, but he didn't brush them away. "And *you* said that *you* didn't want to be that way. You *just* said it, that you didn't want to grow up. And you don't even act like you care. You *are* going to grow up and be mean and horrible."

Sam lay back on the bed and put his pillow over his head.

Polly was shocked by Sam's outburst. Sam hardly ever got mad. At first she wanted to get mad back. But something in Sam's wavering voice made her listen. And even though she wanted to tell Sam that he was totally wrong, she knew that he was at least a little right. It did not make her happy.

She sat and looked at Sam. Then she put

her hand gently on his shoulder.

"Sam," she said quietly.

He didn't say anything.

She shook his shoulder. "Sam, I'm sorry."

Still not a word.

"Sam, you're right," she said in a louder voice. "I was being a jerk." Then she added, "I am not going to say it again, so you'd better forgive me *right now*."

Sam took the pillow off his face. His face was still red. He looked at Polly suspiciously. "We're going to go rescue Joe, aren't we?"

Polly sighed. "Yeah, I guess we have to."

Sam smiled. He wiped his nose with his hand.

"So what are we going to do?" he asked. He couldn't think anymore. All his energy had been used up in getting mad.

"We have to make some real plans," said Polly. "We should have started right away. I guess I just couldn't believe that he wouldn't show up again. And I kind of liked being the oldest. Yuck."

"Yeah," said Sam. "I know you did. It was yuckiest for me."

Polly started to pace.

"Think, Sam!" she ordered. "Think about what Joe could have wished for.

"Something about water," she muttered. "Water…water…water. Dolphins, mermaids, sharks, treasure, the *Titanic*, octopuses, squids, desert islands…" She stopped. "Sam. Help me. Don't just stand there. Think of *something*."

"Okay, okay," he said. "Don't get mad at me, too."

"I won't," said Polly. "Just help me!"

Sam squinched his face up in thought.

"He would be captain of something," he said. "Someone in charge. Someone old, like thirty years. Maybe something from his comics?"

"His comics!" exclaimed Polly. "That's a great idea. But where would they be?"

Sam had no idea. He watched Polly gnaw her lip as she thought.

"There's only one thing I can think of,"

said Polly. "Let's hope there's a clue."

Polly went to the closet and pulled out the bottle. It was foggy inside. Polly pulled the parchment out of the neck of the bottle and unrolled it. Inside the parchment was another piece of paper. It was the cover of one of Joe's comic books.

On it was a picture of a fierce-looking man with a wild green beard and fish's tail. He was holding something that looked like a huge fork, and on either side of him was a shark. Behind him loomed a scaly green sea serpent with giant fangs. In watery type were the words NEPTUNE'S REVENGE.

"That's it," said Sam. "That's Joe's wish."

Polly nodded. "You have to be right. I wonder why he didn't come back after a day, though?"

Sam shrugged. "Maybe he never sleeps, so the magic doesn't know it's been night."

"Or maybe he's in big trouble somewhere," said Polly. "Or maybe if you're in the water when your wish happens, it'll stick."

"We could just wish to be wherever he is," suggested Sam.

"I guess so," said Polly doubtfully. "It might work."

"Let's try," said Sam.

They looked out the window at the drizzle.

Polly shrugged. "It's not that bad outside. We better do it now before it gets worse."

"What are we going to tell Mom and Dad?" said Sam.

Polly thought for a moment. Lying was never a good thing. Finally, she made a choice.

"This is an emergency," she said. "Right, Sam?"

Sam nodded. "A terrible emergency."

"Okay," said Polly. "We have to take matters into our own hands. I'm going to tell them that we're playing a game, like hide-and-seek, so that if they don't see us around, that's why."

"That's good," said Sam. "You go tell them."

Sam was peering into the bottle when Polly ran back in a moment later.

"It's fine," she panted. "We'll have to sneak out carefully."

"I'm good at sneaking," said Sam. "Let's go."

"Wait!" said Polly. "You know what we need, Sam?"

Sam shook his head.

"We need disguises!" said Polly.

"Yeah!" said Sam.

Sam put on his bathing suit. Then he found Uncle Ned's old straw hat. Then he put on one of Dad's T-shirts, which hung to his knees.

Polly put on her bathing suit and her favorite T-shirt, which said LIFE'S A BEACH. Over that she tied a towel around her waist and put one over her shoulders like a cape. Another towel was draped over her head.

"You need a cape," she told Sam.

She tied a towel around Sam's neck. Then she dug into her bag of things she'd found along the beach. There was a bunch of seagull feathers. She stuck them into the band around Sam's hat.

"I guess that will do," she said. "Let's go."

Sam carried the bottle as they went outside.

The wind blew furiously. The sand was wet or it would have stung. Gray-and-white clouds boiled overhead, moving in all directions at once as if giant hands were stirring them. Patches of blue showed through here and there, while a light mist of rain and ocean spray filled the air.

Polly clutched her towel to her head. Sam held onto the straw hat. The wind had blown all the feathers out of his hat by the time they climbed over the dune.

"Look," said Polly suddenly.

Sam looked.

On the beach was an old man dressed in tattered blue and green. He danced at the edge of the water, waving his arms and singing. The waves crashed before him, and he danced away from the foam like a kid.

"Weird," said Polly.

They headed in a diagonal away from the strange man. The mist seemed to gather around them like dust, until they could barely see in front of them.

They reached the edge of the ocean and looked up at the sky, searching for a patch of blue or a scrap of sunlight. But everything was shades of gray.

Polly's and Sam's eyes stung from the salt water. Sam felt weighed down by his damp towel cape. Polly was beginning to feel as if she was wrapped in a giant wet rug. The wind got louder.

"Let's go back in," Polly shouted to Sam. Her voice blew back at her.

Sam didn't want to give up. He also did not want to be alone in the clinging mist.

They turned back toward the beach house. They could only just see the outline of it. A figure came dancing toward them, then there was the sound of roaring water.

"Run!" said Polly.

Sam ran as fast as he could. He turned back to see the wave. The crest curled like fingers above his head. Then the edge sparkled with sunlight. Sam raised the bottle. It glowed magical green as the single beam of light caught it.

"We wish to go to where Joe is!" Sam shouted.

Then the fingers of the wave closed over him.

CHAPTER NINE

Sea Search

Sam opened his eyes. The world was all wavy. Nothing seemed solid. It made him dizzy. He remembered the giant wave and not being able to breathe. He rubbed his eyes with his hand.

Then he froze.

He saw something very clearly—a long tentacle with suction cups on it! Slowly, Sam backed away. The tentacle followed him.

Sam froze again. So did the tentacle. It seemed friendly. Sam let his eye travel down the tentacle to see where it led. It went down a little way and then came back up, up, up, right to where Sam was. The tentacle was him! Sam searched his brain for what had tentacles with suction cups. Then he knew—an octopus!

Sam waved his tentacle and looked for the other legs he should have. Sure enough, there they were. Sam counted them carefully. He had exactly eight tentacles. He was *definitely* an octopus.

Now that he knew what he was, he still didn't quite know what to do about it. It was scary to be such a strange creature. But it was also very interesting.

Sam waved his tentacles around for a bit. He started getting a feel for how far they stretched and which way they curled. Then he looked around.

He was in a rocky cave. Outside, the world floated by. Light filtered down through the water in golden beams. It seemed to come from far away.

Shyly, Sam peeked out further. He didn't

want to touch anything—he was afraid that his tentacles would stick. Carefully, he poked the rocky wall. He didn't stick.

Using his legs, Sam pushed his way through the water until he was out of the little cave. He was getting ready to move again when something crashed into him.

Suddenly, everything went dark. Sam tried to push away through the darkness, but he got confused about where his legs were and ended up in a big tangle. Quivering like jelly, he waited to be eaten.

Then he heard a familiar voice.

"What's going on? What are you?"

And then as the octopus ink cleared, the voice gave a shriek: "An octopus! Gross!"

Sam saw the flash of a sparkling tail.

"Polly?" said Sam. "Is that you?" His words sounded loud in his head but weren't even bubbles in the water.

The sparkling tail stopped moving. A head appeared, with masses of dark hair woven with pearls.

"Sam?" said Polly.

"Yes!" said Sam. "It's me! I'm an octopus!"

He wasn't sure how Polly was hearing him, but it felt as if he was talking right into her head.

"Sam!" Polly swam toward him, holding out her arms. Just as she reached him, she stopped. "I really want to hug you," she said. "But I just can't."

She waved her tail at Sam and grinned. "I'm so happy to be a mermaid again! And to swim in the ocean! It's amazing! Don't you love it?"

"Well," said Sam. "Yeah, kind of. It's neat. I had to learn how to move, though. I've got a lot of legs. I haven't figured out everything they can do yet."

"Except get in a big mess," laughed Polly.

Polly reached out to help him get untangled. But the moment she touched his skin, she pulled back.

"You feel very weird," she said, wrinkling her nose again.

"I know," said Sam happily.

"I don't know if I can do this," said Polly, still struggling with the tangle of legs.

"Please?" asked Sam. "My legs are all falling asleep. And they're tingly!"

In the end, Polly helped Sam get untangled by pointing at a tentacle and telling him to slide it one way or another. It was not easy to keep track of which leg was where and exactly how to move it in which direction. But finally, it was done.

"This is so wonderful," said Polly. "Now we can swim together. I can do flips and all sorts of tricks!"

She did a flip to show him.

"Or try this," she said. She slowly turned upside down. Her hair waved around her. It seemed to have grown a lot. She made a silly face.

"Um, Polly," Sam said. He waved his tentacles at her. "Pol, what about Joe?"

"Oh, no!" Polly said, quickly turning right side up. "I totally forgot! We're wasting time!"

"You're telling me," Sam muttered.

"He has to be somewhere pretty close by," Polly went on, "because that's what we wished for. I can't believe I forgot." And with that, she shot gracefully forward.

Sam was stuck trying to figure out how to get all his legs pushing at once. Finally, he started counting. On "one" he pulled his legs in, on "two" he pushed them down, and on "three" he would glide. Then he repeated the whole thing.

"One, two, three. One, two, three." Sam was counting so carefully he didn't notice that Polly had stopped until he crashed into her.

"Watch where you're going," she said.

"But you…" Sam started.

Then he stopped. Polly wasn't paying attention—she was too busy looking around.

"I *know* we wished to be where Joe was," she muttered to herself.

Polly's tail waved back and forth. Sam thought it made her look more like a cat than a mermaid.

Suddenly, a silver wall of fish was flowing around them. Their heads were filled with silver humming and murmuring. Two phrases seemed to be repeated over and over: *the one of the sea is here* and *swim, swim, swim*. Suddenly, the fish were past them.

"What did those fish say?" asked Polly.

"Something about 'the one of the sea' and swimming," said Sam.

"That's it!" said Polly. "I bet 'the one of the sea' is Joe!"

She darted off in a blue-green flash.

Laboriously, Sam followed.

"One, two, three. One, two, three," he counted.

Soon a rocky wall appeared ahead of them. The silver fish flowed over it and disappeared.

"This is about where I found you," said Polly, pointing to the wall.

"I bet Joe's behind there," said Sam.

They swam over it and stopped short.

"Wow," said Polly.

Sam was speechless.

CHAPTER TEN

Water City

*B*efore them was a city. Beautiful but crumbling buildings stretched along wide sandy avenues. In the center of it was a massive stone structure with columns along the front.

Sea creatures filled the water. There were small fish and big fish, fierce fish and fancy fish, jiggling jellyfish and sleek dolphins, shy octopuses and glowing eels. There were stingrays, seahorses, starfish, killer whales, and, of course, sharks.

Slowly, they swam into the crowd. The

humming and murmuring of the sea creatures filled their heads. They carefully avoided sharks, jellyfish, and anything that looked as if it might have sharp teeth or stingers.

Everything was swimming toward the building in the middle. Sea creatures teemed through its giant columns already.

"It looks like a library," said Sam.

"Or like a Greek temple," said Polly. "Or a Roman one."

"Like in our book of myths," said Sam.

"Yeah," said Polly. "But those weren't underwater."

The temple loomed larger and larger. They reached it and swam with millions of tiny fish between massive columns. Slowly, the fish in front of them cleared away. Polly stopped, and Sam bumped into her again.

"Sorry," he said.

"Shhh," said Polly. "Look."

In front of them was a gigantic statue of a man. He had a flowing green beard, a golden fish tail, and a giant spiked fork. The statue filled the space. It was enormous.

Sam and Polly stared at the statue. The huge blue-green eyes seemed to swirl. Sam started to feel dizzy.

Suddenly, a rumbling sound filled the sea. The water trembled. Something flickered behind the statue's head, and a huge snake's head appeared. It glittered with scales that were all the colors of the sea. A forked tongue flicked past a pair of fangs, each one longer than Sam.

"Sea serpent," Sam whispered.

Its body seemed to go on forever. Its shiny eyes glowed. Scary as it was, Polly found herself thinking, *How beautiful!*

Around Polly and Sam, all the sea creatures sank to the floor of the temple.

Sam and Polly looked at each other. Then they lowered themselves to the floor on top of a pile of eels. Polly muffled a scream. Sam wondered what eel tasted like.

A huge voice echoed through the water.

"Um, hi, everybody," it said. "How ya doing?"

Sam and Polly looked at each other. What was going on? The eels beneath them shifted uneasily.

"Um, okay," boomed the majestic voice. "You may rise and, um, go. And don't eat each other till you get home."

Slowly, all the sea creatures rose. Then a discontented murmur rippled through the crowd.

"That's all," echoed the voice, squeaking a little at the end.

But instead of swimming off, the sea creatures moved toward the sea serpent.

"Hey, what's going on?" said the sea serpent nervously. "Get on out of here. Shoo!"

Sam and Polly looked at each other. "Joe," they said. They both started to giggle.

The serpent bared its fangs at the approaching sea creatures. It twitched its tail and thwacked the statue's head.

"Ouch!" boomed Joe the sea serpent.

The sea creatures began circling him

menacingly. Sam stopped laughing. It looked as if Joe was in trouble!

"Polly," said Sam. "He needs help!"

Polly was almost hidden by her bubbles of laughter.

The sea serpent was now shrieking. "Stop! Go away! Leave me alone!"

Polly struggled to pull herself together. Finally, she took a deep breath and held it. Much as she liked laughing, she didn't want anything bad to happen to Joe. Getting eaten by a bunch of angry fish would be horrible.

"Joe!" Sam shouted. "Joe! It's me—Sam." He pushed his way toward the serpent.

Polly was right behind him. "Leave him alone!" she snapped as she pushed fish and crabs and jellyfish out of the way.

Sam and Polly kept yelling as they swam toward the tightly coiled sea serpent. They pushed their way through the crowds of fish. Sam was having a hard time shouting and swimming at the same time. He kept wanting to count inside his head instead of shouting, "Joe! It's me!"

The sea creatures continued to hum words in angry tones. They surrounded the serpent and hummed more and more furiously. The sound completely drowned out Sam and Polly.

Finally, they made it all the way through the crowd of sea creatures. They both stopped, not wanting to get closer to the serpent's fangs. Sam wrapped a tentacle around Polly's hand. He felt her fingers hold tight. Then they swam right up to the serpent's head.

The serpent's eyes were squeezed shut.

"Joe," cried Polly. "It's us!"

But the serpent didn't even open its eyes.

"I think he's too scared," said Sam.

"What a baby," said Polly.

"Let's whisper in his ear," said Sam.

"Okay," said Polly. "Do you see an ear anywhere?"

"No," Sam replied, "but we can whisper right beside his head."

"You do it," said Polly.

"No, you," said Sam.

"No, you!" said Polly.

Suddenly, something pushed them apart.

"Ahhh!" they both yelled as the serpent's tongue flicked from one of them to the other.

"Can't you guys ever shut up?" said a booming voice. "Why do I always have to come along and keep things moving? Geez, what would you do without me?"

"Joe!" screamed Polly and Sam. They threw their arms, all ten of them, around his scaly neck. "We came to save you!"

"I don't need to be saved," Joe said irritably. "I've been doing just fine."

"Yeah, right!" said Polly. "We heard you: 'uh, er, um, hi, everyone'!"

"I just need some practice," grumbled Joe. "I hate talking in front of people. After all, the only thing I've been the boss of before is you two."

"Oh, brother." Polly rolled her eyes. "Like you're our boss…"

Just then, a new roaring filled the temple.

The serpent, mermaid, and octopus looked around. The fish and other sea creatures had dropped back to the ground. The water trembled around them. Then a crack ran down the statue's face and one of its giant eyes winked.

CHAPTER ELEVEN

King of the Sea

The statue's other eye blinked. Bits of stone drifted down onto the underwater crowd. A giant fist crushed stone to dust. Giant shoulders shrugged away heavy slabs. Giant feet shifted and giant toes wiggled in their sandals. Finally, a giant head shook a shower of shards in all directions.

The living statue stretched his arms and yawned.

"By Zeus," he said, "I hate being so big."

The voice wasn't booming, like the serpent's. It was smooth and rolling, like waves on a calm day. None of the kids spoke, but they moved closer together. Sam wrapped one tentacle around Polly's hand, and another touched Joe's scaly body.

The giant seaman's eyes looked in their direction.

"It's very impressive, though, isn't it?" he said.

The octopus, mermaid, and sea serpent nodded their heads in agreement.

"You're impressed enough now, aren't you?" the seaman asked.

The kids nodded again.

"Hey," said Polly. "I know who you are! You were the weird guy dancing on the beach!"

The man gave a rolling laugh. He lifted his giant fork and struck the ground. There was a golden flash and a BOOM and the man disappeared. In his place was a dolphin.

"Ah, much better," said the dolphin. It wiggled in delight.

The kids felt better, too.

"Who are you?" asked Polly.

"Some call me King of the Sea," said the dolphin. "The names that might be most familiar to you are Neptune or Poseidon."

"So you're a god?" asked Joe.

"Yes and no," said the dolphin. "I am neither god nor human, animal nor spirit, male nor female. I am always here, and only time and the moon can change me."

"That sounds like a riddle," accused Polly. "Not an answer."

"I love riddles and games," said the dolphin, "and contests, too. Humans seem to be the only ones who appreciate those things. Well, my family likes them, but none of us are good losers." The dolphin paused.

"What's the matter?" asked Sam.

"Let me tell you a story," said the dolphin. "Several thousand years ago, I lost a contest with one of my nieces over a little city. They even named the city after her. *Athens*. I haven't talked to her since."

"Well, that's just silly," said Polly. "You just

have to get over it. Especially if you're the older one. I forgive Sam all the time."

Sam rolled his eyes.

"It was such a nice little city, though," said the dolphin. "I wanted them to name it after me."

Joe rolled his serpent eyes. "Come on, man. How long ago was it? Give it up."

"I can't help it if I'm moody," growled the dolphin. "It's my nature."

"Whatever," said Polly. "You've got to go make up with your niece."

"It's the mature thing to do," said Joe.

Sam reached out a tentacle to the dolphin. "You'll be a lot happier," he said.

"I suppose you are right," said the dolphin. Then he laughed. "Now I've got to go find her. Where could she be? This will be a great challenge."

"Hey," said Joe. "What about us?"

"What about you?" said the dolphin.

"You sent the bottle, didn't you?" Joe asked.

The dolphin laughed again. He really was

moody. "Yes," he said. "I wanted some time off. I knew that once word of my waking went around, everything in the sea would be headed this way to tell me all their problems. It happens every time."

"So you sent the bottle out because you didn't want to do your job?" said Joe.

"So I like to take a break now and then," said the dolphin defensively. "Besides, I sent the bottle out with directions to find the one who most wanted to be me at the moment. And that was you. Not that you did a very good job of it. Only three days, and you stir up a hurricane by storming around randomly…"

"But I didn't know what to do," protested Joe. "It's not like you left me directions."

"No initiative, no sense, no maturity," the dolphin went on, ignoring Joe. "That's the problem with kids nowadays."

"It's not his fault that he didn't do a great job," said Polly. "You set him up. You didn't help him at all."

"Yeah," echoed Sam. "It's not his fault."

"Who are you to be talking about maturity?" said Polly.

"No kidding," said Joe. "You didn't want to do your own job and used magic so you wouldn't have to."

"I couldn't have done it if you hadn't been willing to make that wish," said the dolphin with a smirk. "Besides, you didn't think you needed help, did you?"

The sea serpent looked away.

"Leave him alone," said Polly.

Joe raised his giant serpent head. "He's right," he said. "I'd been reading about Neptune, King of the Sea, in my comic book. He was so cool because he was, like, *king. I* wanted to be king." He fell silent. "And what do I turn into? A sea serpent! I spent days just swimming around the city, trying to figure out what I really was. Shouldn't I look like the statue if I wished to be King of the Sea?"

"The king takes many shapes. You took the one most suited to your disposition," said the dolphin. "Someday you'll understand."

"I hate it when people talk that way," said Joe.

"I hate it when *you* talk that way," said Polly.

"Me too," said Sam.

"I don't talk that way," said Joe in surprise.

"Oh, yes, you do," said Polly. "Right, Sam?"

"Yeah," said Sam. "All the time. And Polly did it when you were gone."

The dolphin started swimming away purposefully, singing to himself.

Polly recited a list of Joe's failings. "You're bossy. You act like you know everything. You pretend you're a grownup. You took the bottle when you knew we'd been chasing it. And then you stole a wish!"

"Okay, okay...I'm sorry," said Joe before Polly could go on. "But you and Sam always leave me out."

"What do you mean?" asked Polly.

The dolphin disappeared between the columns of the temple.

"You and Sam stole the bottle from my

room and made a wish without me," he said.

"But you *never* want to play with us," said Sam.

"How do you know?" asked Joe. "Do you ask? *Nooooo*, you only come get me when you need help."

Sam and Polly shifted uncomfortably.

Joe looked around. "Hey, where'd he go?"

Polly and Sam looked around, too.

"How are we going to get home?" wailed Sam.

"See," said Joe, "I'll have to save you again."

"No," said Polly. "We have to save each other. Don't forget that Sam and I saved *you*, even if you won't admit it."

Joe was silent for a moment. "Oh, all right. There were some things I shouldn't have done. And you did save me, kind of."

"And you saved me the day we found the bottle," said Sam. "And I'm sorry I don't ask you to play, even if you would say no most of the time."

Polly sighed. "And I'm sorry that we left you out. And I guess you saved me the first time I was a mermaid."

Joe ignored Polly's tone of voice. "It's a truce then?" he said. "We'll call it even?"

Polly and Sam nodded.

The water around them shivered. The temple started melting away in ripples. Then the sandy bottom of the sea started rising. It made Polly, Sam, and Joe feel dizzy. Then, suddenly, they couldn't breathe. They all kicked their way up toward the beams of sunlight.

One by one, they bobbed up to the surface, gasping for breath and blinking in the dazzling sun that sparkled off the water. They had one moment to look at each other before a wave hit them.

Not again, thought Sam as he swallowed water.

But the wave gently picked them up and put them back on the shore beside the green bottle.

CHAPTER TWELVE

Water Proof

"*I*t's just like one of those books where people learn things that are good for them," Polly said in disgust. "Everything gets better when we agree with each other."

"Look, Pol!" said Sam. "There's your sand castle! And our towels. And our beach chairs. They weren't there when we left."

The kids stared at their stuff. Then they looked at each other.

"Maybe it's Monday again," said Polly.

Sam picked up the bottle, and they walked

over to their towels. Joe picked up his watch. He looked at the date on the watch face.

"Monday it is," he said.

They all looked out at the sea.

"I think we helped him," said Polly.

"I don't know," said Joe. "I did his job badly for a few days, and now he's going off to find his niece instead of doing his job. I think that's a bit irresponsible."

"We can't all be as grown-up as you," said Polly with a grin. "Even god grownups need to play sometimes."

"Hey," said Joe. "I play. Don't tell me that I don't play. Just because you're always playing..." Then he saw Sam and Polly giggling. He laughed with them.

"Someday you will understand," Sam intoned.

Polly and Joe both jumped on him and began tickling him. Sam shrieked with laughter, and the world had returned to normal.

Later, Sam didn't even want to take off his

bathing suit. He was afraid of forgetting the adventure. But Mom said that it needed to be washed.

Inside the little pocket in the front was a small, flat object. He pulled it out.

A coin gleamed green and blue in his hand. It was the same color as the god's eyes. Around the edges was a design. It was the same wave design that he had seen on the magic parchment. And it moved the same way, too. But this time, it didn't make him dizzy. It just made him smile.

Polly pulled her T-shirt over her head. As she did, something fell to the floor. She felt around, then picked up something tiny and round. She held it up to the light. It was a pearl.

Joe's Neptune comic book was too wet to be saved. With a sigh he tossed it into the wastepaper basket. It made a loud *thunk* that did not sound like a wet comic book at all.

Joe reached into the basket and pulled out a rock. It was smooth and gray and shaped like a leaping dolphin. It looked wet. But it was actually dry to his touch.

Dad called out that it was time for dinner. Joe put the rock into his jeans pocket as he ran upstairs.

After dinner, the kids gathered quietly in Joe's room. They showed each other what they had found.

"The magic broke its own rule," Polly said. "We weren't supposed to be able to take anything with us."

"Maybe being given something is different than wishing for it," said Sam.

"I think Neptune's admitting that he's not perfect either," said Polly. "Just like us."

"Speak for yourself," said Joe, but he was smiling.

They examined the bottle. It was filled with seawater. It looked like an ordinary bottle. The parchment was gone. But they had proof that the magic had happened.

That night, the sea sang them to sleep.

The rest of the week passed *again*, this time

uneventfully and without strange weather.

The kids kept the bottle on hand, just in case, but nothing more happened. It was almost a relief.

The grownups didn't seem to notice that the week was happening all over again. Nor did they notice that Joe had disappeared completely for nearly three days.

Before breakfast on their last day, Sam, Polly, and Joe made a decision. They wrote a message on a piece of notebook paper. Sam picked up the bottle. Joe put on his new sunglasses.

"Where are you going?" Mom asked as the kids trooped past her. She was sorting the laundry with Uncle Ned.

"We're putting a message in a bottle," said Joe.

"And we're going to throw it into the sea," said Polly.

"For someone to find," finished Sam.

"Sounds like fun," said Mom. Her hand went to the shell pendant she always wore around her neck. She looked at Uncle Ned. "When Ned and I were kids, we found a message in a bottle with your dad. That's actually when I met your father. Remember, Ned?"

"Of course," said Uncle Ned. He smiled down at Little Ed. Or was he smiling at the wavy silver ring on his finger?

"You'd better hurry," said Dad, coming down the stairs. "We've got to eat before we go."

The kids ran down to the beach. They stopped at the edge of the waves.

Polly handed the paper to Sam. He slid it into the bottle. He handed the bottle to Polly.

Polly pushed the cork into place and banged on it to make it secure. She passed the bottle to Joe.

He held the bottle in his hand for a long moment. Then he looked at Polly and handed it back to her.

She grinned. Then she drew her arm back and snapped it forward.

The bottle sailed through the air. It went

beyond where the waves were breaking and was gone.

The kids didn't move or speak. Finally, a wave washed over their feet.

The water lifted foam-tipped fingers from the sand and waved at them. "Good-bye," it laughed quietly.

"Did you hear that?" asked Polly.

Her brothers nodded.

"I'm glad we wrote the note," said Sam.

"So am I," said Polly.

"I wonder if he made up with his niece," said Sam.

"I guess we'll never know," said Joe.

They turned back to the house, each of them holding their gift from the sea. Joe was aware of the warm sand beneath his feet. Sam felt the sun on his face. Polly was thinking hard.

"I just know he'll do it again someday," she said.

"What?" asked Joe.

"Wake up and not want to be a grownup,"

said Polly. "And find a way to get out of it for a moment."

"I think I'll do that when I grow up," said Sam.

"Me too," laughed Polly.

Joe was silent. He looked at his brother and sister. He took the dolphin rock out of his pocket and held it. It seemed to wiggle.

"Me *three*," he said.

Far beneath the sea, the water shivered.

Dear Water Element,
Thank you!
Sam
Polly
Joe

Don't miss the next book in

The Magic Elements Quartet

when Polly and Sam find another message

and another mystery in

Earth Magic

MALLORY LOEHR lives in Brooklyn, New York, and doesn't go to the beach often enough. When she was a kid, her family went to Nags Head in North Carolina for a week every summer. Some of her favorite books growing up were by Edward Eager, C. S. Lewis, Zilpha Keatley Snyder, and Lloyd Alexander. She spends her free time reading, writing, painting her apartment, and imagining what she would wish for if she got three wishes.